THE LIFELONG MISSIONARY

THE LIFELONG MISSIONARY

Matthew Dohyer

ISBN 978-1-105-33594-5

To the Monday night group

Mark was running out of time to witness to the man sitting next to him on the airplane. The man was wearing a polo shirt and had the casual impatience of a regular traveler. He had his headphones on and was watching the end of a movie on the screen in the seat in front of him. Mark reproached himself for not starting a conversation during the first hour of the flight, while the man had been reading. He knew that he should talk to the man about God. After all, if he had good news, he should be happy to share it. Somehow though, he always felt uncomfortable trying. He had kept a Bible in his hands since the beginning of the flight, hoping the man would ask him about it, but the man said nothing. Not knowing what to do, he thumbed through the Bible looking at different passages, waiting for one to catch his interest.

The flight was from Costa Rica, where Mark had spent five months studying Spanish, to Lima, Peru, where he was going to be missionary. He had hoped to end up sitting next to a Peruvian, or at least a native Spanish speaker. Instead, the man he was placed next to was clearly American, and by the accent he used when talking to the stewardess, seemed to be from New England. In the last five months, Mark had hardly talked to any Americans who weren't missionaries, and he felt he had half forgotten how to talk to an ordinary American.

The man left his headphones on through the credits of the movie, and Mark began to despair that God would give him another chance to witness to him. When the man finally removed his headphones, Mark tried to make eye contact, but the man wouldn't look over. Mark took a breath, steeled himself, and began:

"So, I was wondering if I could talk to you about something."

The man eyed Mark suspiciously, glancing at the Bible in Mark's hand.

"What about?"

Mark looked down at his Bible, then in the direction of the man's knees, and said, "Did you know that God has a plan for your life?"

The man closed his eyes, put the back of his head against the headrest, and let out a sigh. Mark felt he should have had a normal conversation and gotten to know the man first, but he had already started his presentation.

"In Jeremiah," he continued, opening his Bible, though not looking at it, "it says, 'For I know the plans I have for you, declares the Lord, plans for ...'"

"Yeah, yeah, yeah," the man interrupted. "I've heard this all before. Get to your point."

"I just wanted to talk about God's perfect plan for your life," said Mark.

The man turned to Mark. "I guess you want me to convert to your religion, huh?"

"That's not what I was going to ..."

"Good," the man interrupted sarcastically. "So I don't have to accept your religion. That's a relief."

"But I just wanted to share God's plan with you," said Mark meekly. "Don't you want to know what that is?"

"I'd rather not hear what you think God's plan is. I already went through that indoctrination every Sunday as a kid and finally had to learn for myself never to let anyone tell me what God wants me to do."

The man leaned back in his seat again, and as he put his headphones back on he said, "I'd appreciate if you let me enjoy the rest of the flight in peace."

Mark decided it was best not to try interrupting the man, even though he clearly wasn't listening to anything on the headphones. He wondered if it would have been better if he hadn't said anything. He had come on too strong, he knew that, but he found it especially difficult to talk to Americans about God. He hoped the Peruvians would be more responsive.

When they disembarked and got into the gate, Mark walked slowly to let the man get ahead so they would no longer need to actively ignore each other.

I

Mark walked awkwardly to the center of the reception area of the Lima airport. He was wearing two backpacks and dragging a suitcase. Hundreds of people pressed against a waist-high metal railing that blocked off the large open area from all but those exiting customs. Most were restlessly examining the new arrivals, several were shouting out names, having recognized the people they were looking for, and a few were holding up signs with people's names. Mark turned around, trying to get his bearings as the high ceiling reflected the sounds of the shifting crowd, blurring them together into a tinny roar.

Mark suddenly realized he had been hearing his name off to his right. He turned and recognized the mission field director standing in the crowd waving his hand in the air. Having only seen pictures of him on the mission Web site, the director's big smile seemed out of place on his face. Mark squeezed through the crowd at a gap in the metal fence to get to the director. He held out his hand to greet him, but the director tried to give him a hug around the two backpacks and said, "Hello, Mark! My name's Bob. Welcome to Peru!"

The director introduced his wife to the new missionary, but Mark hardly heard, being overwhelmed by the chaotic crowd. They grabbed his luggage and squeezed their way through the crowd, with the director in the lead fending off exorbitant offers from taxi drivers.

As they passed through the automatic doors, the noise inside the airport died out, replaced by the sounds of the parking lot and distant highway. The sun was out, but the air was hazy and there were two massive billboards at the back of the parking lot, blocking the view in order to declare the superiority of specific shoe and cell phone brands. Mark had expected to feel an emotional rush upon finally entering Peru to start his life's work, but this sight, at least, wasn't enchanting.

They walked to the director's blue SUV and put Mark's luggage in the back. As Mark sat down in the back seat, he noticed how new and clean the gray upholstered seats were. Most people wore seat belts in Costa Rica, but he wasn't sure what the Peruvian custom was, so he decided to wear his seat belts until he found out.

As they turned onto the highway, Mark still felt strangely disconnected as he saw his first sights of the streets of Lima through the window. The buildings on either side of the highway were only a few stories high, and everything seemed to have a thin coat of gray dust on it.

"So here's the plan," said the director. "Tonight you'll be at our place; tomorrow we'll move you to your new apartment. You'll then have a week to rest and get adjusted, and then we'll start talking about what you will be doing here. How are you feeling?"

"A little tired," said Mark. He stared at the buildings going by the window, trying to evoke some sort of emotional response.

"You can rest some when we get to our house," the director said. "We'll take you out to dinner tonight if you want."

They drove in silence for a while, and Mark watched the traffic they were weaving through. Most of the vehicles were four-door sedans, many with taxi signs mounted on the roofs or windshields. They passed a small, white bus with the names of various streets painted on the side. It had stopped to let off passengers. He felt a sudden, sharp longing as he turned around to see the bus pass behind them. He wanted to be on the bus, full of Peruvians, as one of them. The longing faded away as the bus disappeared in the traffic.

"What do you think?" asked the director, waving his hand at the buildings and traffic.

"Um … it doesn't look too different from Costa Rica," said Mark, "though the roofs are all flat here."

"That's 'cause we're in a desert," said the director. "We have no need for slanted roofs."

The buildings suddenly ended, and they had an open view looking down a steep dirt slope to the ocean a few hundred feet below. The road veered off to the left and down the side of the slope and, after one switchback, continued next to the ocean itself. As they continued, the slope steepened until it was a dry brown cliff made of compressed dirt and large rocks, looming over the road.

"I thought I'd take the Circuito de Playas, since it has the best view," said the director.

For a while, the road was next to the water, a hundred feet from the base of the cliff wall. There was an orange plastic webbed fence blocking off an unused road right next to the cliff. The unused road had piles of dirt and rocks in various places where it had fallen from the cliffs. On entering another district of Lima, the cliffs weren't as steep but were covered with green vines that had small, dark purple flowers. The district had apparently decided to spend the money to water them.

They passed a couple gravelly beaches beyond which surfers in wetsuits floated in the water. Shortly after passing a restaurant sitting on its own small peninsula in the ocean, they made a U-turn and then started up a gap in the cliffs. They passed under a bridge that spanned the gap from one corner of the cliff to the other. The car bounced around as it went up a stone-paved road. They were entering Miraflores, the section of town where the director lived.

Mark noticed the many tall, new skyscrapers and how comparatively clean the buildings and streets looked. There were more skyscrapers than there had been in San José, Costa Rica. Still, the skyline didn't feel as grand as that of Minneapolis, where Mark's family went a couple times a year to visit relatives, and certainly fell far short of Chicago, close to where Mark went to college.

They entered a neighborhood and pulled up to the director's house. It was a beautiful, white, two-story house, though where a white picket fence would be expected, there was a fence of eight-foot-tall steel bars with spikes along the top. The anti-theft walls Mark had seen in San José were rougher, using broken glass and barbed wire on top of walls—poor people protecting their few possessions—but this one looked professional and expensive. He eyed the spikes suspiciously. It seemed if you had to worry so much about protecting your stuff, it was because you had made an idol of it. The director honked his horn. After a minute, the garage door—a single, solid panel made of wood—was swiveled back and up along its track by a rope attached to the inside of the door. The rope was being pulled by a short, smiling, middle-aged Peruvian woman who was wearing jeans and a light pink blouse.

After getting out of the car, the director introduced Mark to the Peruvian woman.

"Nice to meet you, Mark," she said in English with a strong accent.

"Guadalupe is our maid and cook," explained the director as Mark leaned forward to let her right cheek touch his in the traditional greeting kiss. "She works here on weekdays and has prepared a room for you to stay in tonight."

Some of the students in Costa Rica had maids, as did a couple of the Costa Rican teachers. That had always made Mark feel uneasy, but to see the director with a maid really bothered him. He thought it sad to see a Peruvian, someone they should be trying to reach out to, stooping to the position of being a servant to American missionaries. What message did that send?

Mark tried not to show this disappointment as he replied in Spanish, "*Mucho gusto*, Guadalupe."

As they took Mark's luggage to the guest room on the second floor of the house, the director gave a brief tour, showing the bathroom, kitchen, dining room, and living room. Mark was amazed by the new furniture, new appliances, big-screen TV, and spacious kitchen.

"Would you like to head out to dinner in a couple of hours?" asked the director after they had placed the luggage in the guest room.

"Sure," said Mark.

"You can rest until then. If you want to send an e-mail home, you can use our computer, or if you have a laptop, you can use that, since we have wireless. If you need anything else, let us know."

"I think I'll rest for now," said Mark.

"Okay. I'll come and get you when we're ready to head out to dinner," said the director.

Mark shut the door and sat on the bed. He opened his backpack and pulled out a small poster with a map of the world. He stared at it, letting it sink in that he was south of the equator. After twenty-two years of life and preparation, Mark had finally made it to Peru, where God had called him to be a lifelong missionary. Many of his friends had said they felt called to be missionaries, but he had actually done it. He closed his eyes and remembered his friends from the church high school group sitting around the campfire at the end of a youth barbeque. They had just returned from a two-week mission trip in Europe and they told everyone, with an almost crazed look in their eyes, that they felt God had called them to be missionaries, but Mark knew that their excitement wouldn't last much longer than the campfire. They were easily excitable, and their superficial passions of being called would burn out quickly, not having any true commitment to sustain them. By the end of fall semester, where their intense passion had once been, there would remain only dead coals.

Mark's hero, Nathan, who had left to be a missionary in Ukraine three years before Mark, had warned him this would happen. People passionate about missions would be sucked into complacency, never finding a convenient time to set out on the path to being a missionary. He could see them in his mind in their old age, having lived comfortable, insignificant lives in America, like so much gravel in a dead parking lot. He had vowed not to let this happen to him. He would let nothing stop him from being a lifelong missionary. His whole life, Mark had been pushing himself towards this, feeling like some force was waiting, should he delay, to trap him in America and expose him as having lived a life no better than his peers. And now that he was in Peru, finally starting on the journey that would take the rest of his life, he felt he could relax a little.

He took off his shoes and lay down under the covers. After setting the timer on his watch to wake him in forty-five minutes, he threw his arm over his eyes to block the light from the window, and went to sleep. When the timer went off, he woke up just enough to set it for another seven minutes, and then lay in a blissful half-sleep.

When it went off the second time, he slowly got out of bed. It was getting darker outside. Mark walked quietly out of the room and down the stairs in his socks. He felt calm and clearheaded, and his warm clothes made it almost feel like he was still dreaming in bed. At the foot of the stairs, the living room was silent and peaceful; to open his mouth would be to ruin it. The lights in the living room were on, but they seemed pathetic compared to the light of the lowering evening sun, which passed through the windows and left orange rectangles on the black leather couch.

Mark walked into the kitchen, found the cups, and figured out the switch on the water filter attached to the faucet. Carrying the cup without yet taking a sip, he walked through the living room to the office. The director was seated at the computer and, when he saw Mark walk in, he turned and said, smiling, "Well, it looks like our new missionary is up."

Mark slowly opened his mouth and then said quietly, trying not to break the mood, "I was wondering if I could send off some e-mails."

"Certainly," said the director, standing up. "Do whatever you need to. Yell if you need anything."

Mark sent a quick e-mail to his family and supporter list saying that he had arrived in Peru without any problems. He then wrote a separate, longer e-mail to Nathan, telling him about his flight, his excitement for finally having arrived, and his shock at the director's fancy house.

Mark felt a closer connection to Nathan than he did to any of his other friends. When he went on his first mission trip in high school, Nathan, who was in college at the time, had been one of the leaders. They worked on building a house in a border town in Mexico for a week with twenty other high-school kids, but Mark was disappointed that they stayed separate from the Mexicans, never entering one of their houses. Even the church service they had was run by Americans, not Mexicans. On the fourth night, he found himself sitting next to Nathan at the campfire. The fire lit up Nathan's face and jeans, but his black T-shirt was hardly visible against the night behind him. Mark had watched him from a distance through the beginning of the trip, a little intimidated by Nathan's age and height, as well as from the maturity and quiet self-confidence he showed.

"How are you liking the trip so far?" Nathan had asked.

"I'm glad to be out of the United States, but I was hoping to spend more time with the Mexicans," said Mark.

"I know what you mean," said Nathan, "but that's how most short trips are. You know, a lot of kids can't handle more than this, but at least they get some experience of another culture, right?"

"I guess so," said Mark, "but I had been hoping for more. When I head out as a real missionary, I'll make sure I don't get stuck hanging out with Americans the whole time."

"Yeah, I'm the same way. I want to be *involved* with the culture when I'm a missionary."

"You want to be a missionary too?" asked Mark.

"Yeah man, as soon as I'm done with college next year," said Nathan. "I can hardly wait."

"Well, I still have to go through all four years of college before I can go off to Peru, where I want to plant churches and show people God's plan. Where do you want to go?"

"I want to share Jesus's love in Eastern Europe," said Nathan. "I haven't figured out which country yet, but it should be awesome."

"So you wouldn't happen to be interested in going to Peru, would you?"

"Nah, I don't think my calling is for Peru," said Nathan.

"I guess there are people in all foreign countries that need to be told God's will."

"Yeah, people everywhere need Jesus."

"Yep," said Mark. "Have you learned any central European languages?"

They spent hours that night, along with much of the rest of their time in Mexico, dreaming about how they would do missions.

Over the next year, they spent time together regularly to share their enthusiasm about missions. Mark introduced Nathan to Keith Green's songs about missions, and Nathan would read from missionary biographies. They loved reading about Hudson Taylor's success in the 1800s after he went against the other missionaries by wearing his hair in a long braid and dressing in a robe like the Chinese he worked with.

At the end of that school year, when Mark went out to start at Wheaton College, he was sad to part with Nathan. Whenever he was back on vacation from school, they made sure to spend time together, catching up and dreaming about mission work. When Nathan finished his studies, he left to be a missionary in the Ukraine during Mark's sophomore year of college. Mark faithfully, and with a bit of envy, read all of Nathan's updates from the mission field and kept in contact with him through e-mail.

Now Mark was finally able to send his first e-mail to Nathan, not from the United States, but from out in the world as a fellow missionary.

Mark sent the e-mail, logged off, and walked to the living room with his cup still full of water. It was now dark outside, and the director had closed the curtains. Mark sat on the couch in front of the TV, which was off. The director's wife walked through the room shortly after.

"Will you be ready to go out for dinner in a little while?" she asked.

"Yep," said Mark.

"Do you mind if we invite some of our other missionaries?" she asked.

"That would be fine," said Mark, though he would have liked to have been able to meet more Peruvians.

The director's wife grabbed the remote and handed it to Mark, saying, "You can watch TV until we're ready to leave if you want."

"That's okay," said Mark. "I don't really like TV anyway."

He leaned into the corner of the couch so he wouldn't have to face the large blank TV and drank his cup of water.

After a few minutes, the director came in and told Mark that it was time to leave. He grabbed his shoes from his room and got in the back seat of the SUV. The director backed out while his wife waited in the garage. She closed the garage door behind them and a minute later came out the front door and got in the car.

"We're going to Larco Mar, a nice mall overlooking the ocean. There are a bunch of restaurants to choose from, and we can see what you're hungry for," said the director as he drove.

Night made the houses and skyscrapers they drove past seem even grander and cleaner. When they got to Larco Mar, they drove into the underground parking lot and found a spot. As they were walking towards the mall entrance, the director spotted the missionary family he had invited. He introduced Mark to the family. The father was in charge of evangelism at one of the mission's churches, his wife taught at an international school, and they had a nine-year-old daughter and seven-year-old son. They passed between a bookstore and a Starbucks and onto a walkway. The walkway went along the whole east side of the mall and overlooked a large plaza with restaurants. Beyond that, to the west, was the empty darkness, where the ocean lay. Mark looked over all the restaurants and stores, but when he looked to the right, he was horrified to see a Hooters on the bottom level. *So this is what we've given the world,* he thought sadly.

"We've got American fast food below us," said the director. "Tony Roma's over there, ice cream in front there, and a couple Peruvian restaurants. What are you hungry for?"

"Well," said Mark. "Since I'm in Peru, I'd like to try some Peruvian food."

They walked toward a restaurant that was above the Hooters, passing clothes stores, jewelry stores, and a Radio Shack. At the guardrail at the west end of the mall, they stopped to look out over the ocean. The mall was built into the side of the dirt cliff that lined the ocean. A hundred feet below them traffic snaked along the road at the base of the cliff. Mark could only see the ocean in a few places; the rest was a black expanse that merged with the black sky. The two kids stepped onto the bars and lifted themselves up so they could poke their heads over the top rail. On the left, a hill extended out into the ocean. On the hill sat a giant cross of white lights that reflected off the ocean water, allowing Mark to see the waves coming in. He looked away, feeling uncomfortable with the unsubtle sign. It seemed strange to turn a symbol of suffering into something so bright and garish. Mark stared straight out into the blank night. The air felt cold, fresh, and natural while the waves rumbled against the shore.

"The view here is great, isn't it?" asked the director.

"Yes, it is," said Mark.

"You ready to eat?" asked the director.

"I guess so," said Mark.

As they turned around, Mark was again confronted by the bright, opulent sights of the mall. They sat down at a table next to the restaurant and about twenty feet from the guardrail. Mark sat at one end of the table, next to the evangelism leader and across from the director. The director's wife sat next to the director, and at the other end of the table the two kids were being taken care of by their mother. Next to the table was an eight-foot-high movable stand with a lamp-shaped heater on top, warming the air. The waitress came up, dropped off the menus, and said in clear English, "Welcome! My name is María. I will be your waitress tonight. I will return in a little bit."

Mark started looking through the menu. The meals were listed in Spanish, but he was disappointed to see that the descriptions were in English. *When am I going to get to use the Spanish I just spent five months studying?* thought Mark.

He turned to the drinks and asked, "Are there any drinks that are particularly Peruvian?"

"Yeah, there are several," said the evangelism leader. "The main non-alcoholic ones are Inca Kola, the Peruvian soda, and *chicha morada*, which is a juice made from purple corn."

When the waitress came again, Mark ordered in Spanish.

"*Me gustaría una Inca Kola*," he said carefully.

The waitress smiled at him and then continued taking everyone else's orders in English.

As they waited for their drinks, Mark began asking for suggestions on Peruvian food.

"Well, there's a lot of fish, since we are living on the coast," said the director.

"You'll have to try *cebiche* sometime," suggested the director's wife.

"Is that the raw fish?" asked Mark, making a face in spite of himself.

"Yeah, but it's really good. One of my absolute favorites," said the evangelism leader. "Don't be scared to eat it just 'cause it's raw. The lemon and onion kill off the bacteria. If you're going to live in Peru, you have to try it at least once."

"I wasn't trying to sound like I didn't want raw fish. I really want to try it," said Mark. "If it's authentic Peruvian, I want to try it."

"Well, don't get it tonight," said the evangelism leader's wife. "Since it's caught in the mornings and not cooked, Peruvians never eat it after lunch."

"I'll have to remember that. What else is there that's particularly Peruvian?" asked Mark.

The director and the father gave a number of suggestions. Mark ended up deciding on *dorado a lo macho* since it sounded like something unusual.

After a few minutes, the waitress came with their drinks. The waitress asked if they were ready to order, and Mark again ordered in Spanish while the others ordered in English. When the waitress left, Mark tried the bright yellow Inca Kola while the two kids ripped off one end of their straw wrappers and blew into the straw, shooting the rest of the wrappers at their mother. The Inca Kola tasted a bit like bubble gum.

"So how long are you planning on being in Peru?" the evangelism leader asked.

"I've been called to be a lifelong missionary," said Mark, "so I plan on never leaving. You can bury me here when I die."

"Wow," said the evangelism leader. "I've been here for eight years and I'm still not sure that I want to be here forever. Anyway, I was going to ask if you are interested in being involved with evangelism at our church in El Centro."

"Which church is that?" asked Mark.

"That would be *Divino Redentor*, a church we started in downtown Lima," said the director. "We'll go there tomorrow."

"That's the poorer section of Lima, right?" asked Mark.

"Yep," said the director.

"Then I'm looking forward to visiting."

"Definitely," said the evangelism leader. "A lot of our missionaries go to that church, and I'm in charge of the evangelism program there. So if you ever want to go out with us to do evangelism ..."

"I don't know," said Mark cautiously. "I'm not sure yet what programs I want to be part of."

"Don't have to worry about it now," interjected the evangelism leader's wife. "You just arrived today. Where in the States are you from, Mark?"

"I'm from Minnesota, about an hour northwest of Minneapolis."

"And where'd you go to college?" she asked.

"Wheaton," said Mark.

"Wheaton? That's a good school," said the evangelism leader. "I would've liked to go there, but I couldn't afford it, so I went to a community college. But I didn't have to take out loans, which made it a lot easier to come here."

"Actually, that isn't a problem. Wheaton now has a deal where they will pay off a quarter of your student loans each year you are a missionary if you go straight into missions. So I don't have to worry about my loans."

"Huh," said the evangelism leader. "So if you stay here for four years ..."

"Actually, I've only got three and a half years before Wheaton pays off the last of my debts, since the five months I spent at language school in Costa Rica count too."

"Huh," said the evangelism leader, looking to the side and rubbing his tongue over his molars. "That's sure sounds tempting, but I'd still be afraid to do it."

"Well, I know God has called me to be a lifelong missionary, so I'm not worried."

The evangelism leader turned his eyes back to Mark. "Well, I guess you'd have to be really confident you know God's will to do that."

They returned to the topic of the mission's current work in Peru and, by the time the food arrived, Mark heard all about the evangelism program and the international school.

The waitress set down the plate of food in front of Mark. On the back right corner of the plate was a piece of lettuce that had a few intricately carved vegetables sitting on it. The main dish was a large fillet of fish hardly visible under a yellow sauce full of *mariscos*, which Mark had thought just meant shellfish, but he could see something with suckers on it. As a kid, he hadn't eaten much seafood. He picked up the tentacle first and gingerly took a bite. It was rubbery. As he continued eating, he made sure every bite included some of the fish fillet and he chewed carefully to avoid feeling any suckers.

"How do you like it?" asked the director's wife.

"It's certainly different," said Mark. He'd meant to say it as a compliment, since he had wanted to have something uniquely Peruvian, but his expression made it clear he wasn't enjoying it much.

"Well, it will probably take a while to adjust to the food here. Especially be careful about salads," she warned. "At this restaurant it is safe to eat salad because they clean it well, but be careful elsewhere."

As Mark got towards the end of his meal, he began to feel how exhausted he was. He dropped out of the conversation and let the others keep talking. He watched the two kids split their time between eating their food, playing with their food, and arguing with each other and their mom. Mark made sure to finish all the food that was on his plate, but he noticed that the two kids only got halfway through their food and let the waitress take back the plates.

Mark nearly fell asleep on the ride back to the director's house, and when they arrived he went straight to bed.

The next morning, a warm and sunny Sunday, Mark watched the buildings pass by out of the SUV window with growing excitement as they transformed from modern homes and glass skyscrapers to the graffitied walls and ornate constructions of El Centro. This was the Peru Mark had imagined himself working in.

The church was a yellow, two-story building, the facade flush with the sidewalk and the neighboring buildings. A large sign above the door declared, "The Church of the Divino Redentor." A Peruvian man handed Mark a bulletin as they walked into the building. There was a pulpit in the center of the stage, and off to the right of the pulpit a guitarist, bass player, drummer, and singer were getting set up. Two sets of pews faced the front of the church. Mark followed the director and his wife down the center aisle and into one of the rows on the right. The director introduced Mark to the family sitting in front of them. Their names were Roberto and Paola, and the pastor of the church was Roberto's uncle. Mark beamed as the director explained that he was a new missionary who had come to work in Peru. Another Peruvian family came in and sat down to Mark's left. He said, "*Hola*," and they politely returned his greeting. Mark, not sure what was proper for small talk in Peru, didn't try to continue talking to them. The pastor then came up to welcome everyone, and the band started playing the first song.

Mark knew most of the songs, as most of them were translated American worship songs. All he had to do was make sure he used the Spanish words on the screen in place of the English ones. There were only two songs that he didn't know from English, and one of these he had learned in Costa Rica. Before the last song, the offering plates were passed around, and then it was time for the sermon.

Mark tried hard to understand what Pastor Guillermo was saying, but the Peruvian accent threw him off. He caught snippets of thoughts and was able to figure out which Bible verses were being used, but he couldn't put it together enough to know what exactly the point of the sermon was. He found himself looking around, instead of listening, noticing how the pulpit, pews, band, and dressed-up congregation all felt very much like an American church.

After the service, everyone stood up, and Mark Roberto and Paola turned around to talk.

"I hope you enjoyed the service," said Roberto.

"Sí," said Mark. "Though I had difficulty understanding it all."

"In time," said Paola, "you will understand better."

"Does the church have many events for young people?"

"There's a youth group the church has Friday nights," said Paola.

"I should go," said Mark.

"Unfortunately," cut in the director, "our mission prayer meetings are then, so Mark can't attend."

"So I can't skip some of the prayer meetings?"

"No," said the director. "That you cannot do."

"There's also a Bible study before the service," said Paola. "Some of the youth go to that."

Mark glanced at the director, who nodded in approval.

"I'd like to go. When is it?"

"It starts one hour before the service, at nine in the morning," said Paola.

They continued talking for a few minutes before the director and his wife took Mark out to lunch.

After lunch, they loaded all of Mark's stuff into the back of the SUV and went to Mark's new apartment.

The apartment was on the fourth floor of a ten-story apartment building. It had a living room, kitchen, office, bedroom, and bathroom. Overall it was a spacious, well-furnished apartment, and the director informed Mark that it was only a fifteen-minute walk from Larco Mar. After bringing up Mark's luggage, making a pathetically small pile in the middle of the living room, the director took Mark on errands. They first went to Movistar, a Peruvian cell phone company, so Mark could get his own Peruvian number, and then to Metro, a large supermarket just like one in the United States, except over the cash registers were TVs playing music videos for those in line. After buying enough food for Mark to survive on for a few days, the director returned Mark to his apartment to let him settle in.

"Anything else you need for today?" asked the director.

"I think I'm okay," said Mark.

"Then I'll stop by tomorrow afternoon to check up on you," he said, leaving Mark alone in the new apartment.

Mark took the groceries to the kitchen and sorted them out into the refrigerator and cabinets. He crumpled the plastic bags into a ball, put them in an empty drawer, and returned to the living room. Sitting on the couch to recover his thoughts, he found himself staring at a blank TV screen. He unplugged the TV and turned it so it faced the wall, then moved the couch and chairs so that the TV was no longer the focus of the room.

Mark dragged his backpacks and suitcase to the bedroom and emptied their contents on the floor. He put up his small poster of the world on the wall in the bedroom and put away his clothes, toiletries, books, CDs, and computer. With everything put away, there was hardly a visible mark to show this was Mark's apartment and not some model room shown to potential renters.

After spending Monday morning uneventfully wandering around Miraflores without introducing himself to anyone, he decided he should go Tuesday to El Centro, where the church was. When the director stopped by that afternoon, Mark got the directions to give a taxi to get to the church.

He went to El Centro Tuesday morning and wandered around, trying to memorize the street names and what was on them. As he ate a late lunch at a small restaurant, he enjoyed watching the Peruvians interact, and after lunch he noticed a group of guys who seemed about his age playing soccer on a concrete courtyard in a school. The older ones were wearing casual clothes, while the younger ones still wore their school uniforms. He stopped and watched for a minute. Being unsure if it was acceptable to just walk up and ask to join a game, he left without saying anything.

Mark spent Wednesday trying to get a feel for his neighborhood in Miraflores, but after spending a day in El Centro, he noticed how much lighter skin the people in Miraflores had. There were more foreigners wandering the streets, and the Peruvians themselves were dressed like American businessmen and college students. Mark wanted to work with the more authentic and less Americanized Peruvians in El Centro.

On Thursday, after eating at one of the many Chinese restaurants in El Centro, Mark found the guys playing soccer at the school again and built up enough courage to go up and ask to join. The entrance to the school building was a twenty-foot-long solid metal door that had been swung open inward. Mark passed through this into the courtyard and walked to the sideline.

"Hola!" said Mark. "Can I play with you?"

The guys paused their game, looked at each other questioningly, then turned back to Mark and replied, "Claro." *Of course.*

One of the guys came forward, introduced himself as José, and asked Mark to play for his team. He was tall for a Peruvian, a little taller than Mark, and had darker skin than the other players. José introduced Mark to the other players on the team, Mirko, Ademir, Julio, and Pedro, though Mark had trouble remembering who was who.

During the game Mark was only able to understand the more basic phrases the others yelled to each other. When they shouted more complicated instructions or started bantering, he had no idea what they were saying. Pastor Guillermo had been hard to follow, but when they got going, it felt like another language entirely. Still, Mark was happy to be playing with them, and he played reasonably well, seldom losing the ball and even managing to steal it a few times.

In the end, Mark's team lost by two goals and the other members of his team started pulling out loose change. He asked what they were doing and, with some difficulty, they explained that Mark owed the other team fifty cents. When he told them that he hadn't known they were playing for money, they laughed and said, "Bien vivo eres!" *You're very alive!*

Mark asked what that meant, and they said that he was being tricky and trying to get out of paying. He tried to defend himself, telling them he would never lie or trick them intentionally, but they just laughed and accepted his fifty *céntimos.*

They told him that they played at the same time, 3:00, every weekday. Though Mark was uncomfortable playing for money, he promised to be back again the next day.

Mark left immediately after playing soccer the next day so that he could get back to his apartment, shower, take another taxi, and be at the director's house on time for prayer meeting.

Six other adults, besides the director and his wife, along with several children were at the house when Mark arrived promptly at 6:30. The director welcomed him in and introduced him to the families that had already arrived. Two of the couples were missionaries from the United States, but the third couple, Rodolfo and Gloria, was from Ecuador. Mark was glad that not everyone there was an American. After the introductions, the director told him he could grab some snacks in the dining room and visit until the others arrived.

The snack table was full of familiar foods: brownies, popcorn, pie, and vegetables with dip. The only things that looked unfamiliar were small glass bowls that held a purple Jell-O-looking substance with cinnamon sprinkled on top. Mark asked one of the other missionaries and found out that it was a traditional Peruvian desert called *mazamorra morada*, which was made from purple corn, just like chicha morada.

Mark picked up one of the bowls and began to eat it. There were chunks in it that turned out to be fruit, though some of them had seeds inside. Mark looked around and saw someone else almost done with a bowl and no sign of the seeds, so Mark swallowed them whole, figuring that's what he was supposed to do.

Another family arrived and was briefly introduced to Mark. He then stood back to eat and watched the other missionaries catch up with each other. Two of the American guys were talking about some American football game they had recently seen, several of the women were discussing how to organize an upcoming school event, and the kids were running around making noise.

By this point Mark had eaten most of the mazamorra. He had found a particularly large seed and was trying to decide if he was willing to swallow it when he saw the other missionary who had been eating the mazamorra morada walk over to the trash can and dump the seeds that had been hidden in his hand into the trash.

Families slowly trickled in until 6:50, when the director finally announced that they would start the prayer meeting. Chairs were placed around the director's living room, and everyone found a seat.

One of the missionaries, a man about thirty years old who had come with his wife and three young children, pulled out a guitar and led the group in worship songs. Mark was disappointed that they were all in English and looked over to see the Ecuadorian couple singing along in English. During the third song the evangelism leader and his family came in the door and went to the back of the room. Mark wondered why he had bothered leaving soccer so quickly when no one seemed to worry about showing up late to prayer meeting.

After the songs, Rodolfo, the Ecuadorian missionary, came forward and talked for a bit about what he found meaningful in some psalm. Mark found it strange that he would use English. Everyone there spoke Spanish, right? Why then do they put on the farce of acting like they only speak English? Especially the Ecuadorian missionary. His English was fluent, though he still had an accent, and Mark imagined that he would have been more comfortable giving his devotion in Spanish.

The Ecuadorian missionary asked for prayer requests. He said a brief prayer to start, then let others take turns, and finally said a closing prayer. The director came up, thanked everyone for coming, and invited everyone to return to the dining room for more snacks.

After Mark grabbed a second mazamorra morada, the evangelism leader came over and asked him how he liked his new apartment.

"I'm surprised how big and nice it is," said Mark, trying not to sound like that was disappointing.

"I'm sure you'll like it," said the evangelism leader eagerly. "And how did you like the church?"

"I had trouble understanding the sermon, but I'm excited about getting involved in El Centro."

"Remember, if you are interested in the evangelism program there, just talk to me."

"I will."

For the next forty-five minutes, Mark found himself having to repeatedly answer questions from the other missionaries about his family and how he had ended up in Peru. Finally the director offered to give Mark a ride back to his apartment, which Mark was grateful for.

On Sunday after church, the director took Mark to a cheap Italian restaurant in El Centro to work on Mark's goals in Peru.

"So," began the director, "my job basically is to manage all our missionaries in Peru. I try to make sure each person knows what they are trying to do and then keep up on how they are doing. I believe you said in your application that you wanted to work with discipleship and evangelism. So now that you've been here a week and had a chance to see some of what we're doing and meet some of the missionaries, what do you think?"

"I still am interested in discipleship and evangelism, and I really like being in El Centro," said Mark, looking out at the noisy street. "I want to get involved in the neighborhood here."

"You mean with people from the church?" asked the director.

"Yes," said Mark. "But also with the normal people who live here. You know, playing soccer, eating at the restaurants ... just hanging out in general."

"And you said you've already started playing soccer here, right?" said the director.

"Well, only a couple times so far. But I want to keep doing that," said Mark. "After I get to know them better, maybe I could invite them to a Bible study."

"At the church?"

"I would try to invite them to the youth group on Friday nights if I could get out of the prayer meeting."

"Well, I'm not letting you get out of prayer meeting," said the director. "That's the one time all our missionaries get together."

"Then I would want to start my own Bible study for them," said Mark.

"That would be good."

"You know," ventured Mark, "it would be a lot easier if I was living in El Centro."

The director smiled, exhaling through his nose, and rubbed his eye behind his glasses. "Yeah, it probably would. But as a missionary, there is a difficult balance between convenience for ministry and safety."

Mark wondered how much the director balanced these. "So, could I move to El Centro?"

"No," said the director. "At least not yet. You need to have lived here for some time before you could be safe there."

Mark had been waiting the whole week to ask that question and was disappointed by how quickly it was shot down.

"How do you see your involvement with Divino Redentor?" asked the director.

"Well, I went to the Bible study before church today."

"How was that?" asked the director.

"I was able to follow along better since I could figure out what verse we were looking at."

"Well, as your Spanish improves, that will get better," said the director. "Have you made friends with anyone in the Bible study?"

"I met a few of the guys my age, and I want to start hanging out with them as well."

They spent the next hour setting down specific goals for Mark. The main goals were to attend church and continue playing soccer in

El Centro at least three times a week, as well as thinking about how he could start a Bible study there. In one month's time he was to report back to the director about how it went.

Of the goals they set for the month, soccer went the best, with Mark playing four or five times a week. The fact that the *fútbol* games were for money made him uncomfortable, especially when he felt culpable for his team's losses. But he told himself it wasn't really gambling since, like professional sports, it was based on skill and performance, not chance. Mark continued playing every weekday and felt himself becoming part of their group of friends. He was thankful for his straight, black hair and his relatively short stature because, though he still stood out as a gringo, he blended in better than most other gringos would.

Mark began hanging out with the other players after fútbol, especially with José and Pedro. Despite several missionaries' warnings, he felt comfortable walking through downtown with them until well after dark. The times he spent hanging out with them after sunset were the times he felt his friendship with them grow the most. One evening, after Mark had treated them to Chinese food for dinner, they walked around the little shops, looking at hats and jewelry. José suggested that Mark get a bracelet with light green stones on it, and when Mark checked and saw that both José and Pedro also had bracelets (José's was a thin band with a cross on it, and Pedro's was made of orange stones), Mark bought it and wore it proudly as a sign of being one of them.

The long taxi rides back to his apartment gave Mark plenty of time to think about how much more convenient it would be if he lived downtown near them. All the friends he made, both from church and fútbol, lived there. The commute back and forth from Miraflores seemed like a waste of time. He began speaking openly of his desire to move downtown to the other missionaries. They were skeptical, warning of the dangers of El Centro, but what type of missionary avoids his calling because it might be dangerous?

He began to make it a point to regularly ask the director when he could move downtown. After much discussion, the director relented and agreed to investigate the possibility. After another month, with Mark continually reporting his progress, the director gave Mark a lengthy speech on how to keep a low profile and keep himself from being a target; then he cautiously announced to Mark that he had found a suitable, safe apartment for him to live in. *Well*, thought Mark, pleased, *I guess the director's all right.*

II

On the second Monday in March, after completing two months in Peru, Mark moved into his new apartment. The director had offered to help him move, but since Mark had few possessions, he just got a taxi to take him there. By now he knew that those in the passenger seat in Peru were required to wear seat belts while those in the back weren't. He sat in the back since he preferred to ride without a seat belt.

The director had taken Mark to see the building the week before, so he knew the way. When they arrived at the building, Mark first went into the office to get the key, and then the taxi driver helped him get his stuff up to the room on the second floor. Mark paid the driver a little extra for helping carry his luggage.

After the driver left, Mark started a CD of Spanish music on a cheap CD player he had bought in Miraflores. Since arriving in Peru, he had stopped listening to English music, wanting to immerse himself in Spanish.

He unpacked his belongings and began putting them away in the new apartment. It had a similar arrangement to the one in Miraflores, and was only a little smaller. It was fully furnished as well, but the furniture looked lightly used, unlike the new furniture at his former apartment. This apartment still didn't seem to fit Mark's personality, but when he walked over to the window and saw El Centro, he felt like he could make himself at home here.

After he finished unpacking, he sat down on the couch and wrote in his journal about how he was finally living among the people he would work with and all the hopes he had of making disciples among his new neighbors.

While lying in bed that night, Mark listened to the new, unfamiliar sounds outside. There was the noise of traffic and distant loud music from parties. In the middle of the night he heard two loud bangs. He couldn't tell if they were fireworks, gunshots, or something else, and he wondered if he should get up and do something about it. He couldn't think of any useful course of action, so he tried not to feel guilty about doing nothing and eventually fell asleep, focusing instead on all the things he would do for God while living in El Centro.

Mark woke up the next morning with a sore throat; his mouth tasted like smog. He tried to go back to sleep, hoping the sore throat would go away, but after an hour he decided sleep wasn't helping.

He dressed and went to the little store across the street, where he bought a box of orange juice. A cart was on the sidewalk in front of the store selling bread and cheese. He bought some rolls and some of the "fresh" cheese, which was a type of cheese that hadn't been given time to dry. On returning to his apartment, he drank a glass of the orange juice, but it didn't help his throat. Mark cut a roll and put in a slice of the cheese. He took one bite but didn't like the taste or feel of the moist, salty cheese, so he put the sandwich in the microwave to melt the cheese and found it much improved. After finishing the rolls and cheese, he left the apartment.

Uncertain of where to go, he began walking down the street he lived on, observing all he could. The buildings looked old, and the paint had thin splotches of dark gray grime, especially around corners and moldings. The skyline was full of old skyscrapers, and many looked abandoned. There was a lot of traffic, and each street had its own personality. One street had ten rotisserie chicken restaurants all in a row; others were small, trash-covered roads with visibly decaying brick walls. There were many permanent stands set up on the streets, some selling bottled water and drinks and others selling tabloids that had inappropriate pictures of women on the covers. The people generally looked poorer than in Miraflores, and there were some homeless people lying on the sidewalk. Mark passed a beggar and asked himself what he should do. He didn't want to support drug or alcohol abuse, but he also didn't want to be stingy. He couldn't decide before he passed, so he walked by and tried not to make eye contact with the man. Mark felt the man's eyes follow him, as if the man could see through his back and right into his soul.

Mark hadn't seen any of his friends, so after a few blocks he turned around and walked back the other way, looking for someone to talk to. He came to a large market covered with a metal roof that took up a full block. The market was organized into rows of garage-like rooms that had been converted into various shops. He walked through them, past rows of clothing shops and toyshops before he came to a large open area in the center, where the roof was highest. The area was filled with aisles of tables full of fresh fruit, vegetables, and meat. The smell of raw meat was not something Mark found pleasant, so he went off in another direction and found a row of shops selling food and drinks. He picked one and ordered a pineapple juice, giving him the opportunity to talk to the lady selling it. He felt that, as this was his first day living among these people, he should start up a conversation about God.

The shop had a small counter with three stools, all there was room for. After the woman had finished making the juice by mixing water, sugar, and fresh pineapple in a blender, Mark asked if she believed in God.

She replied, "Claro." *Of course.*

After a little more prodding he found out she was a Catholic, honored the saints, and even had a small alter to a saint in her home. Mark was bothered by her idolatry—following saints instead of God's plan. He tried to explain to her what the Bible said about idolatry, but she wouldn't listen. She quickly labeled him as an *evangélico* and seemed to think that ended the argument. Mark kept arguing, but finally, deciding he wasn't getting anywhere, he paid and left before he realized he hadn't even asked her name.

He went back to his building and up the four flights of stairs to his apartment, where he sat on his couch, thinking through his plans for the day. He kept checking his watch until 12:15, when he thought it finally late enough to get lunch. But even then, all the restaurants were closed, and he wandered around for another twenty minutes before he found a clean restaurant that was open.

The restaurant had a number of small square tables that fit four people. The restaurant had recently opened, so most of the tables were empty. Mark sat at a table by himself. He would have preferred to sit at a table with other Peruvians, but he wasn't sure if it was culturally appropriate to join a table of strangers, and he didn't have enough confidence to just go up and ask. He ordered the $2 *menú*, which came with a salad, a bowl of soup, a plate of rice with chicken, and a drink. Mark finished his food quickly, since he didn't have anyone to talk to, and then he paid and walked over to the school to wait for fútbol.

When he arrived at the school, the last of the school kids were leaving, so he sat on the concrete bleachers next to the field to wait for the others. Eventually the other guys arrived, and they played two games, both of which Mark's team won. After they finished, they sat down on the bleachers to relax and talk.

"That was a beautiful goal you made, José. It's just sad it was against your own team," said Julio.

"Bueno, I only wanted to make sure that the goal of my friend Mark was necessary for our victory," said José, patting Mark on the shoulder.

"Thanks for making my goal important," said Mark, smiling. "I don't know if you are interested, but I'm going to have a Bible study in my apartment this Thursday at 7:00 if you want to come."

"A Bible study?" asked Pedro.

"Sí, we will talk about what the Bible says. Want to come?"

"Sí," said José confidently. "It would be beautiful to talk about the Bible."

"Bueno," said Mark, relieved that they wanted to come. "It will be in my apartment—two blocks south, then three blocks east. The building is light green and has a blue door, and it's next to the tall gray building. I'm in apartment number 217. Are you all coming?"

"Claro que sí," they replied. *Of course we will.*

Mark was excited that they were all coming, so he spent the next two days meticulously planning his Bible study on idolatry, buying Spanish Bibles, and practicing saying everything in Spanish.

On Thursday, after playing fútbol, Mark ate supper alone in his apartment and set everything up for the Bible study. He had extra Bibles, Inca Kola, and Oreo-like *Casino* cookies sitting out on the coffee table. Spanish worship music was playing in the background. He was excited for the chance to invite his local friends into his apartment, though he was still ashamed to be living in such a big, nice place. Mark had put his laptop and camera in his bedroom and closed the door because he didn't want to show off his wealth. He wouldn't have brought a laptop at all if it hadn't been a gift from a supporter that he felt obligated to use.

At 7:00 PM he sat down on the couch facing the door, ready for his friends to ring the bell. He expected them to show up between 7:15 and 7:30. He tried to relax and listen to the music, but he was too nervous and excited. Since he hadn't had anyone over before, he wasn't confident the bell worked, so he kept walking over to his window to see if anyone was coming. The entrance was right below his window, so he had to stick his head out the window to see.

At 7:30, no one had arrived. At 7:45, Mark opened the first package of cookies. By 8:00 he had eaten most of the cookies and was staring at a half-empty three-liter bottle of Inca Kola, wishing he had someone to talk to.

Mark didn't feel like leaving the apartment that night and quietly went to bed. He woke up the next morning and threw away the cookie wrappers and used plastic cup and put the now-flat Inca Kola in the fridge. He forced himself to leave the apartment to get breakfast, but after eating he found himself returning to his apartment again.

That afternoon he went to the fútbol game, and while he played he tried to forget that none of them had come and to act like everything was fine. After the game was over, they sat down to talk for a bit before playing again. He didn't want to offend his friends, so he decided not to bring up the subject of the Bible study. After talking about what had happened in the game, José asked, "Did you have that Bible study last night?"

"In truth, no one showed," said Mark.

"Are you going to do it again? Possibly you'll have more next time."

"I'd like to try again next week," said Mark. "Would you like to come?"

"Claro," said José.

As the conversation moved back to fútbol, Mark ran over the conversation in his head. How was José not sure that the Bible study was going to happen? He had invited them and made sure they knew where he lived. He could think of nothing ambiguous in his invitation or their responses. Mark wondered what José saying he would come this time meant.

It was Friday, so after fútbol Mark had to go across town to Miraflores to attend the prayer meeting. Having lived outside of Miraflores for most of a week, he felt like an outsider at the meeting, not participating, just observing. It made him upset to see all the expensive possessions in the house and to know that they had a personal maid. The only thing Mark could think of that they needed to make their high-class lives complete was a butler. Mark had also found out that most of the other missionaries lived in similar conditions, probably higher-class lifestyles than they had had in America. They had left the United States, but instead of escaping the dead parking lot that was America, they were now spreading it in

Peru. He watched them close their eyes and sing about their love for Jesus while sitting on the beautiful leather couches in the expensive gringo house. The more emotional they were, sometimes with tears in their eyes, the more upset Mark became. After all, hadn't Jesus been homeless? God didn't want Christians to be comfortable, but to make great sacrifices in following Him.

On Sunday, Mark invited some of the guys he had met at Divino Redentor to the Bible study and made sure to remind everyone several times throughout the week. On Thursday, four guys came to the study, two from the church youth, Luis and Carlos, and two from fútbol, José and Pedro.

After everyone was introduced and they had opened a bag of cookies and the Inca Kola, Mark turned to the Ten Commandments and began talking about idolatry. They seemed uneasy, but once he brought up the worship of the saints, Luis jumped on it and started talking about how evil it was. Luis didn't get very far before José disagreed passionately, though Mark couldn't make out what exactly was said. Luis and José continued arguing back and forth, with the others occasionally commenting. Mark caught phrases and words— Mary, the Lord of the Miracles, José's various relatives—but Mark couldn't follow enough to say anything relevant himself. He decided to jump in anyway and regain control. He made them read more verses about idolatry and, after some concluding remarks, opened the rest of the snacks. The Peruvians started conversing and joking with each other, but with all their slang, Mark never figured out the subject of conversation. He found himself simply smiling and nodding as if he knew what they were saying.

After they left, Mark was alone in his quiet apartment and, exhausted from concentrating so hard on the conversations for an hour, he sat down on the couch to relax. He thought the study had gone reasonably well, and he hoped for more success and more people the next week.

The next day was Good Friday, and after a couple games of soccer, Mark's friends sat down on the concrete bleachers to rest and talk. He was able to stay longer with them, as there was no prayer meeting. There was the noise of instruments and a crowd in the distance moving closer, and as it did, his friends got up and walked to the street to see. Down the street was a procession coming toward them.

The procession centered on a large, ornately decorated painting of Jesus dying on the cross.

As it drew nearer, Mark's friends explained to him that the painting was *El Señor de Los Milagros—The Lord of Miracles*. It had been painted hundreds of years ago in Peru by a slave. They said there were many miracles and healings associated with *The Lord of Miracles*, which is why it was venerated so much.

"The *painting* causes miracles?" asked Mark, surprised that they would believe that about what was only a decorated painting, but they all insisted that it did.

The procession was in front of them now. The painting itself was ten feet tall, supported by a large square base being carried by almost twenty people. The base held flowers and candles and seemed to be gilded. The frame was also golden and fanned out about a foot around the painting. A golden crown, dove, sun, moon, cloth, and other symbols were pasted onto the painting as well. The painting itself was dark and hard to see among all the candles, flowers, and gold.

Everyone officially in the procession was wearing dark blue robes. Behind the painting were women with white veils who were burning incense, and behind them was a band playing a somber march with blaring trumpets. Crowds pressed around to see the procession, and many were holding up cameras to take pictures.

Mark was upset and felt he needed to tell his friends.

"We aren't supposed to worship anything physical like paintings—only God," he said.

"We aren't worshipping it, we are venerating it," clarified José.

His friends went to follow the procession, but Mark was uncomfortable with it, so he left them to go get dinner.

After dinner he went to the *Viernes Santo* (Good Friday) service at Divino Redentor. He generally preferred Good Friday services to Easter services, since they felt darker and more serious, and during the service at Divino Redentor, he looked around and was glad to see everyone holding somber expressions.

When the service was over, it was night, and Mark began to walk back to his apartment. He stumbled across another procession, this one with three stands being carried. The first held a cross that was draped with a cloth. The second had a dead Jesus in a glass paneled case, and the last had a mourning Virgin Mary. When Mark arrived at the street the procession was on, the dead Jesus was in front of him. The edges of the glass case were ornately decorated with gold. Each of the four corners had an angel facing out with bowed head. Amidst all this ornate decoration lay the carving of Jesus with smooth, shiny white skin, bloody wounds, and looking like he had been starved before he died. He lay on his back with his eyes closed and his head slightly tilting to one side, as if he might be sleeping peacefully rather than being dead.

Mark felt repulsed, not only by the idolatry of people worshipping manmade carvings, but also at the celebration of death and pain at the center of it. He turned away from the dead Jesus in his glass coffin and tried to focus on the crowd and postulate why they would join such grotesque processions. At least the Mary statue behind him merely looked elegantly sad and not grotesque. Mark was able to look back at that statue and feel sad for the Peruvians who worshiped it.

After the procession had passed, Mark returned home and tried to keep the images of the strange bloody carving of Jesus from coming to his mind.

That Sunday was Easter, and Mark was a little disappointed to see that the members of the church were no longer somber. They had a potluck after the service, for which he had brought Inca Kola. As everyone laughed and ate, Mark wished he could go back to the Good Friday service, where they had seemed to take their faith seriously. He wished there could be more days between Good Friday and Easter to let the seriousness and cost of following God sink in. At least he could impress this view on those who came to his Bible study.

Unfortunately, that Thursday evening Mark started to get sick. He tried to think through all that he had eaten in the last day, but there were a number of things that could have caused it. He had eaten fresh cheese for breakfast and cebiche, the raw fish, for lunch. In the afternoon he had bought a cheap flavored ice that came in a thin plastic bag from a street vendor. For dinner he had eaten cheap Chinese food.

Mark managed to get down the stairs and put a note on the gate apologizing for not being able to do the Bible study, as he was sick. He never knew if anyone came and read the note or not.

That night was the worst of it, but he didn't feel much better on Friday. Mark didn't go to the prayer meeting, and at 8:00 PM, a missionary couple that lived and worked in a nearby orphanage called to see if he was okay. Mark said he wasn't feeling well, and they told him they would stop by.

Mark slowly got out of bed with his pillow, blanket, and a small trash can he kept close by in case he needed to throw up again. He lay resting on the floor as his uneasy stomach settled. He then mustered up his strength, carefully dragged himself into the living room, and pulled himself up onto the couch, where he waited for the couple to arrive.

Eventually he heard a buzz indicating that they were at the entrance gate to the apartment building. He got off the couch, lay on the floor and, as quickly as his stomach would let him, pulled himself to the door. He stood up to press the button unlocking the gate and to unlock the door so they could come in. He then scooted along the floor to the couch and got back in just before they entered.

They had brought crackers, three bottles of red liquid that seemed to be an electrolyte-replacement drink, and two plastic containers of chicken noodle soup. The husband went to the kitchen to heat a small bowl of the soup in the microwave and put the rest in the refrigerator while the wife pulled up a chair next to Mark and asked him about his condition and about what he had eaten. She didn't think it was the cebiche, since he had eaten it at a restaurant she trusted. Instead she suspected that he had food poisoning from either the flavored ice or the Chinese food.

The husband came back with the hot soup and set it on the coffee table next to Mark. Before Mark started eating, the husband put his hand on Mark's shoulder and prayed that Jesus would heal him and help him with his ministry. The husband sat on the couch opposite him, and Mark slowly started eating the soup and crackers. He was glad that they had come by to check up on him and take care of him, but he also wished it could have been a Peruvian family taking care of him.

After leaning forward to eat three spoonfuls of soup, Mark lay back on the couch and closed his eyes.

"How are you feeling? Are you going to be okay eating the soup?" asked the wife.

"Yeah. I think so," said Mark, keeping his eyes closed. "I just can't eat very quickly."

"Well, take your time," she said. "You don't have to rush."

Mark nibbled on a corner of a cracker.

After a minute the husband asked, "So, other than getting sick, how's your experience in Peru been so far?"

Mark cautiously swallowed the bit of cracker that was in his mouth. "It's been okay. I'm working on getting my Bible study going."

"I didn't know you had a Bible study," said the wife. "That can be a very rewarding experience and a good way to get to know the Peruvians. You'll have to keep me updated on it at the prayer meetings. "

Mark ate another spoonful of soup.

The missionary wife looked intently at Mark and said, "I've noticed that you don't volunteer to pray at the prayer meeting, and you leave early."

Mark started to turn to see her more directly and began, "Well, I …"

"Not that there's some rule that says, 'Thou shalt volunteer to pray at prayer meeting,'" interrupted the husband.

"No, of course not," said the wife. "But I was just wondering why."

Mark slowly gathered his thoughts. "I guess I just don't feel comfortable at the prayer meeting. It seems strange to me that everything is in English when we are in Peru and all know Spanish. I feel especially bad for the Ecuadorian couple having to do everything in English."

The husband laughed.

"I actually grew up with Rodolfo when we were both kids in Ecuador. He's glad to have the chance to practice his English since he's surrounded by Spanish during the rest of the week."

"You grew up in Ecuador?" asked Mark.

"I was actually born there," said the husband, "so I am Ecuadorian as well." Mark didn't know what to think about that. "Rodolfo and I both decided to come here to join the work in Lima together, which is where I met my beautiful wife," he said, winking at her.

She looked over at her husband. "Yeah, I was down on a short-term trip shortly after they had moved out here, and by the end of that trip I knew we were going to get married and be missionaries in Peru together."

"Though I was a little slow on the uptake," said the husband, "and it took me another six months to realize I wanted to marry her."

The wife continued looking at her husband for a minute, then turned back to Mark.

"Anyway, is there any way we can help you feel more comfortable at the prayer meeting?"

Mark leaned his head back and closed his eyes.

"I'll think about it."

By Sunday Mark was fully recovered. He held what he considered a very successful Bible study that Thursday. Seven Peruvians attended, and Mark taught on the sixth commandment, "Thou shall not murder," and how that included hatred.

After having that many people, Mark was a little disappointed the next week to have only four in attendance: Carlos, Luis, José, and a guy who looked vaguely Asian called "el Chino." Mark never figured out what his real name was.

Mark started the Bible study by having Luis read the seventh commandment, "Thou shall not commit adultery," and then had them read Matthew 5:27–30 on how that includes "adultery of the heart," which is lust. As Mark explained that any sort of lustful thought was a sin, the Peruvians avoided eye contact and shifted awkwardly.

Mark started giving more concrete examples. "So it is sinful to look at the pictures in the magazines."

"Sí, claro. There are some beautiful women ..." pined José, while the others snickered.

"And women on the street," said Mark.

"Oh, those too," said el Chino. "And at the beach, in the summer ... Ai how beautiful!"

Mark continued, undeterred. "What the Bible says right here is that it is a sin to lust after them."

"But what if the girl is single?" asked Luis, looking sincere.

Carlos said, "The verse says, 'looks at a woman,' not, 'looks at a married woman.'"

"Exactly," said Mark, glad at least Carlos was supporting him. "The Bible says we must not look at any woman lustfully. That's what God demands from us. I know it isn't easy, but God's demands aren't easy. He has asked us to deny our sinful passions and hold every thought captive."

The guys all sat silently, but Mark decided to wait for one of them to say something.

Finally, José looked up at Mark skeptically "And how can that be possible? Because when you see a beautiful girl walking by, like Chino's sister ..."

"Shut up," said el Chino, giving José a quick glare while the others snickered.

"How can you stop yourself from noticing?" finished José

Mark waited to let the weight of the question sink in before looking down at his Bible and reading verse 29. "'If your right eye causes you to fall, pluck it out and cast it away: how much better it is for you to lose one of your members, that your whole body isn't thrown into hell.'"

"You want us to pluck our eyes out?" asked Luis.

"No. I don't think plucking your eyes out would stop lust, but we should fight lust with that much force."

As they continued discussing it, Mark continually reinforced the fact that lust was wrong, and as it became clear that he really believed it, he was pleased to see them get quieter and apparently take it seriously.

After the discussion, while eating snacks and talking of other things, José started prodding Mark about which of the local girls he liked.

"I don't know any girls well," said Mark, trying to get out of answering the question.

José started asking about specific girls that hung around the fútbol games, but Mark kept trying not to answer.

"Do you like girls who are skinnier or more filled out?" asked José, drawing an exaggerated figure in the air, while the others laughed. Mark was upset that Carlos and Luis weren't helping him out.

"Which do you prefer: the indigenous girls, the Asian girls, or the black girls?" asked José.

Seeing that Mark wasn't answering, José leaned over to el Chino and said, "I see now. He must prefer the American gringas."

Mark didn't want them to believe that, so he replied, "Actually, I like Peruvian women more than American women."

"Good! You like the Peruvian women more!" said José with a big grin. "How is being with a Peruvian girl better than being with a gringa?"

"No. That's not what I wanted to say," said Mark. "I like the personalities of Peruvians better."

"Ah, the personalities are different, but being with a gringa is ..."

"No," said Mark, frustrated. "That's not what I'm talking about."

With some effort, Mark finally got them to shift the conversation to the more comfortable subject of fútbol. He was both relieved and discouraged when the guys finally left his apartment, still laughing and joking with each other.

That Monday afternoon, after playing fútbol, José invited Mark to his family's apartment. José introduced him to his mother, Mónica, who promptly offered him coffee. Mark, excited to be there, sat down on one of the couches in their family room and accepted the cup of coffee. He didn't like coffee, but he felt like he was making a big cultural step forward in accepting their hospitality. The room had two comfortable couches, three chairs, a coffee table, and a TV. It was tastefully decorated. There was a curtain at the back of the room, blocking off the rest of the apartment. In future visits, Mark found out the area behind the curtain wasn't as presentable to guests. They hid their poverty behind their curtain like Mark hid his wealth behind his bedroom door.

José then introduced Mark to his other family members: José's younger sister, younger brother, and two nephews. The nephews, Rodrigo and Francis, were sons of José's older brother, Pablo, who was a bus driver and away most of the year. José's father had left when the kids were young. Mónica had raised her children alone, and was now raising her own grandchildren as well. José and his mother watched carefully while Mark was being introduced to José's younger sister, Milagros, who looked about twenty years old. She had very dark skin like José, since the family was of African descent, and was slender and beautiful. Mark tried to be polite without giving the idea he was interested in her. Until he knew whether she was a faithful servant of God, he had no reason to be interested in her. After talking with them a while about what he was hoping to accomplish in Peru, he headed back to his apartment, happy to have finally been invited into an authentic Peruvian home.

Over the next couple months, Mark continued the Bible study, explaining that buying pirated DVDs was stealing, that all lies and deceit were sin, and that wanting too many possessions was a sin. Some weeks no one showed up, but on others there were as many as six. Carlos and José were the most faithful attendees, followed by Luis and Pedro. Mark was glad when they came to the study, but he was frustrated at their inconsistent attendance and their slow progress in accepting and living what he taught them.

Mark tried to find comfort in e-mail updates Nathan sent out. Nathan wrote about the various cultural differences and difficulties he experienced in the Ukraine and how the church he was helping was growing. Nathan always had some story about his Ukrainian friends and their culture. One of Nathan's friends, whose name Nathan kept secret, apparently had connections to the mafia. Nathan had to be careful in hanging out and talking to him, but he seemed interested when Nathan told him about Jesus. Nathan was also working one-on-one, reading through the Bible with several young single guys who had recently been saved. Mark was happy for Nathan's success, but felt like his work in Peru wasn't nearly as successful. He reminded himself he had only been in Peru for four months, while Nathan had been in the Ukraine for almost three years, and he shouldn't expect big results in so short a time. Even if the attendance wasn't consistent, Mark had started his own Bible study. Perhaps in another year, he would also have a booming ministry.

He had figured out enough of the bus system to be able to take a bus to church and even to the prayer meeting in Miraflores, though often he had to take a taxi to get to the prayer meeting in time after fútbol. Mark enjoyed being on the bus, where everyone else was Peruvian. He tried to blend in as best he could and felt like he was a member of the community while he was on the bus.

He was also becoming more fluent and was better able to understand what was being said at church, but he wasn't as involved as he wanted to be. He went on Sundays to the Bible study and service, but he was not able to attend the youth group because of the mission prayer meeting. There weren't any other activities for him to participate in: he didn't play an instrument or sing particularly well; he, of course, couldn't attend the women's meeting; and he wasn't interested in helping with the children's ministry. He could have gone to the evangelism nights, but when he visited he noticed that they had simply translated some American evangelism format that Mark didn't think fit Peru very well. As for what he did attend, the Bible study before the service was a shallow study of the life of Jesus, and Pastor Guillermo's sermons were mostly just gospel presentations. Mark longed for a good, convicting sermon on all the things that a good Christian should be doing.

One Sunday morning early in June, the subject of lust came up during the Bible study before the service. There were about fifteen of them sitting around in a circle. Mark was the only non-Peruvian. After the leader said that now that he was married he refused to look at any other woman, one of the other married guys said to the younger men, "Enjoy those pictures now while you're single, since you can't when you're married."

If Mark was a little more fluent he would have been able to butt in right away. As it was, the conversation was already starting down another path before he managed to cut in. He asked if he had heard right, so one of the others repeated it slowly. Mark, horrified, looked over at Carlos to see what he would say, but Carlos sat quietly, giving no sign of his view. He opened his Bible to *Mateo* 5 and read to them the verses that say anyone who lusts has committed adultery in his heart. The class didn't seem to be sure what the disagreement was, so he said more clearly that any man looking lustfully at any woman was a sin. The class seemed surprised that Mark would say that, and one of the women argued that single guys can't control themselves, since it's in their nature. Mark called it the lie it was:

"*Mentira!* Single guys can control themselves if they want to, but they don't understand the force of their sin. 'If your right eye causes you to fall, pluck it out and cast it away: how much better it is for you to lose one of your members, that your whole body isn't thrown into hell.'"

The argument went back and forth for a while and finally, upset, Mark left the group to tell Pastor Guillermo what was being taught in the Bible study.

Pastor Guillermo was in the sanctuary greeting the families who had arrived. Mark approached him, followed by Carlos and a few others. Mark tried to explain the debate that had occurred and the horror of what the others in the class were saying, but the pastor replied:

"The verses in Mateo talk about adultery, but as long as you are single and the woman is single, how can that be adultery?"

"But adultery includes those who are still single," said Mark.

"And where does it say that in the Bible?" asked the Pastor Guillermo.

Mark couldn't come up with a good reference on the spot and could only say, "Clearly it includes singles."

"I am not so sure about that," said the pastor.

Mark was horrified the pastor was even further in error, and he felt almost helpless. He took a few steps back, looked around, and addressed in Spanish all the people milling around the sanctuary: "Did everybody hear that? The pastor is teaching heresy! He is encouraging people to sin sexually. He must repent!"

The auditorium became utterly silent. The other gringo missionaries looked at him with worried and almost hurt looks.

"If Pastor Guillermo doesn't repent, he must leave the church!"

Pastor Guillermo leaned over and asked Mark what his problem was in a loud whisper: "*Qué te pasa?*"

Mark shouted again to all around him, "This pastor is teaching heresy. He says it is not a sin to lust. Can't you all see?"

The auditorium was silent. Seeing no one would help him, Mark said, "If no one will stand with me, I'm leaving."

Mark turned his back and walked out the door. As Mark passed by, the director asked, "What are you doing?"

Mark replied, without breaking his stride, eyes fixed forward, "What you should have done a long time ago."

Carlos came out behind Mark, but Mark was angry with him for not having supported him. Luis came out a short time later.

"Why didn't you help me?" Mark asked them in a hurt voice and waited for a response, but they made no reply.

After a minute Mark said, "We'll see each other at the Bible study," and walked away to return home.

Three hours after Mark had left the church and returned to his apartment, his cell phone rang. He had suspected the mission director was going to call, but he was not looking forward to talking with him. Mark answered the phone, and the mission director said he wanted to talk at once. It was clear Mark wasn't going to get out of it, so he agreed to wait at his apartment.

Mark couldn't sit down for more than a few seconds at a time as he waited for the director to show up. When the director finally came, they sat on the couches facing each other. The director took a big breath and started forcefully with, "I don't know what you were trying to accomplish this morning, but you certainly did not go about it in a constructive manner. We have put ..."

"I cannot let heresy be taught without saying anything," Mark butted in.

The director continued, separating each word for emphasis. "We have put a lot of time and effort over many years into building this church, and ..."

"Judging by the problems this church has, it looks like all your work has been a waste."

The director continued severely, "And what you did this morning won't help anything."

"And what you've been doing has been helping?" asked Mark fiercely.

"You are new to the field, and you don't understand the issues involved. You are used to the problems that show up in American churches, but you haven't learned to deal with the specific Peruvian problems."

"Trust me," said Mark bitterly. "I see the problems in American churches, and I am now seeing the problems that you have let flourish in your Peruvian church. Your job should be to prevent the church from falling into error."

"Should it?" asked the director in English. He continued, "It is easier said than done to keep these problems out of the church."

"Oh, so you took the easier route and let the church teach heresy without complaint?" asked Mark. "You should get rid of that pastor."

"Pastor Guillermo is a godly man who loves Jesus."

"Then why doesn't he listen to Jesus's commands?"

"Pastor Guillermo isn't perfect. He has his sins and errors; every pastor and missionary does. But he knows Jesus and is leading others to know Him."

Mark leaned forward on the couch with a look that made it clear he wasn't going to give in.

"Look," said the director. "Not all our missionaries go to this church, and I will not force you to. In fact, I expect you to leave Divino Redentor and find another church. I just pray that God teaches you some humility."

Mark scowled ahead stiffly, neither wanting to argue, nor wanting to show he accepted the advice.

The director waited for an acknowledgment, and on not getting one, got up and said, "Then I'll see you at prayer meeting on Friday, and I expect to hear where you plan to attend next Sunday."

Mark remained seated and failed to see the director to the door.

III

Mark had to get up in the middle of the night to put on socks and grab another blanket because it was too cold in his apartment. The weather had been slowly getting colder and damper since he had arrived six months earlier in January. He stayed in bed longer than normal when the morning came, keeping warm. With his blanket still wrapped around his shoulders, he got up, grabbed some bread and Swiss cheese, and walked over to the window. Mark had stopped eating the moist "fresh" cheese his friends ate, and now used better, but more expensive, Swiss cheese, which he kept out of sight in his refrigerator. He looked up at the gray sky and then down to the street four stories below.

Everything was gray and wet. Though Lima received almost no rain, lately the ground was damp in the mornings from an overnight drizzle. The dust on the ground that normally went unnoticed became a thin layer of gray mud in the shallow puddles in the street. There were few people out, and those who were had jackets to protect them from the cold mist hanging in the air. Mark looked at his watch. If he was going to make the Sunday service at *Esperanza* church, he would have to get ready quickly.

A month ago, when the director made Mark choose a new church to attend, he had decided to go with one of the missionary couples to a church called Esperanza in Miraflores. He didn't think he would like it, but none of the other churches looked better.

The first week he went to Esperanza, the missionary couple had given him a ride. After that, Mark took taxis or the bus to the church, depending on how much of a hurry he was in. The church was full of well-off Peruvians: businessmen, teachers, doctors, and others with lucrative professions. After observing Esperanza for a month, Mark was more and more frustrated with how American it all felt, so at his Bible study last Thursday, he explained the problems he was seeing.

"All these churches are just like gringo churches," Mark had said.

"What do you mean, like gringo churches?" asked José.

"The gringos started these churches, and the Peruvians have just copied them. They didn't figure out the Peruvian way to do it."

Mark saw they didn't understand, so he continued, "For example, most of the songs are just translated English songs. For example, '*Abre Mis Ojos O Cristo*' was originally 'Open the Eyes of My Heart.'" Mark listed a few more he could think of off the top of his head.

"What about '*Todopoderoso*?'" asked Carlos.

"That one is originally Spanish. I like that one because it's hard to translate into English."

Carlos continued asking about songs. Mark didn't know if many were English or not. José mentioned songs from Catholic Mass, but Mark didn't know them at all.

"Can you not tell which songs are originally English?" asked José.

"A lot of them sound just like American praise choruses," said Mark. "But that's the point. The American missionaries taught the Peruvians to write gringo praise music. You guys should be coming up with your own music."

"I don't know how to write music," said José.

"I'm not saying you are the ones to fix it, only that it's a problem," said Mark. "And there are other problems as well. The services I've seen are all run just like gringo services, songs at the beginning with an offering, and then the sermon with one more song at the end. That's exactly how my church did it at home. Even the buildings and seats look just like the ones in America. My question is, how would a Peruvian run a service?"

"Pastor Guillermo is a Peruvian, and that's how he does it," said Carlos.

"Yes, but he is just copying what the missionaries did. How would you run a church service if you hadn't been influenced by missionaries?" asked Mark.

"If I hadn't been influenced by the missionaries," said Carlos, "I wouldn't be a Christian and wouldn't be running a church service."

Despite Mark's prodding, they couldn't come up with a Peruvian way of running a church service. José brought up Mass, but that was just another style of church service brought over by white people. They suggested some superficial changes to the order, but what Mark wanted was something fundamentally Peruvian. He had invited them to come over Sunday after church so they could discuss what they could do to fix the Peruvian church.

That Bible study had been three days ago, and now Mark continued slowly getting ready for the Esperanza service, but his heart wasn't in it. He kept checking his watch as he went through his morning routine until he was convinced it was too late to go to Esperanza. He sat down on his couch, relieved he wouldn't have to rush back from the service to meet with his friends.

Mark's friends had been less consistent lately in attending the Bible study. Last week it had only been Carlos and José. Another week only Carlos had shown up, and Mark had decided not to do the study. He wondered later if he should have done it anyway with just Carlos. When Luis came to the study two weeks earlier, he told about how everyone at Divino Redentor had been arguing for weeks about what Mark and Pastor Guillermo had said, and how Pastor Guillermo finally gave a sermon explaining why lust is wrong for singles as well. Mark had said that while he was glad Pastor Guillermo had changed his mind, he couldn't imagine how someone could have been made a pastor while holding such views. He wondered what other heretical views Pastor Guillermo held.

Since Mark was skipping church, he went ahead and pulled out his Spanish worship music and Bibles for the meeting. The missionary couple that went to Esperanza called after two hours, asking where he was, so he explained to them that he hadn't gotten up in time to make it.

Mark sat waiting for the guys to show up until 1:00 PM, when he was finally convinced they weren't coming over. He had been planning on going out to eat with them afterwards. He instead made himself a simple lunch of ramen noodles while telling himself that he should leave the apartment.

After eating, checking his e-mail, and doing everything else he could think to do, he left the apartment and walked down the street. He said hi to a few people he knew as he passed, but didn't stop for what would probably be shallow conversations. He finally ate dinner at a seafood restaurant he often went to. He realized he should have brought a book, since it was a lot less awkward to wait for your food alone if you could at least be doing something. When he returned to his apartment, he put in one of his movies, which he had seen several times lately, because it helped him forget his loneliness. Mark wished that one of his friends would stop by, but at the same time he knew how stressful it was when they came over. He felt like he had to entertain them somehow, and he was never fully at ease.

The next day Mark woke up late and went out to eat breakfast. At a loss for what to do, he returned to his apartment and checked his e-mail. He and Nathan had sent a few e-mails to each other about when would be a good time to talk, though they never seemed able to coordinate a definite time. There were a number of e-mails he knew he should respond to, but he wasn't in the mood. After having read all the articles of interest on the Web sites he usually visited, mostly news sites and sites on missions, but also one about upcoming movies, he closed his computer. Over the last few months Mark had been noticing that he slept in more, not having any activities in the mornings or any pressing work. He would spend hours alone in his apartment with nothing to do and go to bed longing for someone to confide in. He made himself a sandwich for lunch and sat down on his couch to eat it. After eating he felt tired, so he lay back and took a nap.

After the nap he forced himself to leave the apartment to find something to do. He walked down to the school where they played soccer, but the gate was closed. Mark's friends had stopped playing soccer as the weather got colder. He kept walking and saw a group of people playing volleyball in a back street, but he didn't know them and wasn't in the mood to make new friends. He returned to his apartment and grabbed a spoon and a jar of peanut butter he had bought in the supermarket. He sat down on his couch and hit "play" on his CD player. A Spanish worship song began, but Mark turned it off before it got to the chorus. He went to his room and pulled out his favorite Keith Green CD, skipped to track seven, and sat back on the couch with his eyes closed to listen to Keith Green's forceful piano and passionate voice. Though he felt too apathetic to sing along out loud, he silently mouthed the words of the chorus with the CD:

> Jesus commands us to go,
> It should be the exception if we stay.
> It's no wonder we're moving so slow,
> When God's children refuse to obey,
> Feeling so called to stay.

He had listened to this song on his cassette player many times while growing up. Keith Green had said, "If you don't go, you need a specific calling from God to stay home," and Mark knew he wasn't called to stay in America and that he was going to go out to do great things for God. Whenever he heard stories of missionaries from his parents or from church, he saw the sense of longing he felt as a confirmation of his calling. He felt he had a special identification with them and never doubted God also wanted to use him in a mighty way in missions. It had sounded easy then, but nothing seemed to be working out the way Mark wanted it to; he was meeting with so much resistance from those around him. Were these just trials he had to go through before everything fell into place? Was God sending him through a time of testing to prove his resolve? He wished for a sign to comfort him and let him know he was doing the right thing, but it all felt muddled.

Mark had finished the first spoonful of peanut butter. He liked the feel of the peanut butter and cool metal on his tongue, and he absentmindedly dipped the spoon in again. He wouldn't give up. Maybe he was supposed to try harder, or maybe he was just supposed to endure. If depression and loneliness were the price of being a good missionary, he would have to pay it. If he was faithful to God, he knew God would be faithful and provide what he needed. Mark looked around at his apartment again; the main room was spacious and fairly bare. His most expensive possessions, his laptop, CDs, camera, books, etc., were hidden in his room while the main room had furniture and the CD player. It still looked too wealthy. The furniture was high quality; it all matched the curtains and paint, and looked new. He saw now that he had not entirely escaped the American dead gravel lifestyle; he needed to step out farther to escape it. Mark needed to make a greater sacrifice to reach out to his Peruvian friends. He thought how living in a cheaper apartment would make his friends much more comfortable if he invited them over. That would be one less barrier between them. He resolved to head out the next day and start a search for a better apartment, one that didn't have an intimidating gate his friends had to pass through to see him.

In the meantime, he had finished off another two spoons of peanut butter and missed the next several tracks on the CD. He reached over and turned off the CD player before "Create in Me a Clean Heart" could start. He closed his eyes again, trying to find some comfort to carry him through.

The apartment Mark found was much smaller and felt more comparable to what his friends had. It wasn't furnished, and he would have to buy everything from tables, couches, and the bed to light bulbs and curtains. He couldn't take those things from his current apartment, since they belonged to the landlord. There were also a number of problems in the new apartment that would need to be fixed: the toilet didn't work very well, there was no hot water, and the floor was rather uneven. Mark was extremely pleased.

He had told his friends about it that Thursday at the Bible study. The apartment was closer to José's apartment and Mark thought he would've been excited about this, but he wasn't.

"That's a dangerous part of town," José had said.

"But you live one block away. You don't seem like you're in danger," said Mark.

"Yes, but I'm not a gringo."

"I wish I wasn't," said Mark.

He moved in anyway that Friday. He bought used furniture so he could spend the night. When he went to the prayer meeting that night, he apologized again for not going to Esperanza last Sunday and promised to make it the next. He didn't tell any of the missionaries about his new apartment, since he didn't think they would approve.

On Sunday, he made sure to go to the Esperanza service and chatted briefly with the missionary couple. He had invited the guys over again after lunch to talk about church plans, but only José came. They didn't talk much about church, but mostly about the new apartment. When José asked how much it cost, Mark still felt ashamed as he answered, since he knew José's apartment housed more people and was probably cheaper still. Mark started talking about all the difficulties of living in the new apartment. He laughingly explained how he had to heat up water on his stove in order to attempt a warm bucket shower.

"That's how we shower in our home," said José.

"Oh," said Mark, suddenly ashamed. He realized he had been boasting.

That week, Mark spent quite a bit of time outside. He found new places to eat near his new apartment, but he didn't know anyone, so he ate in silence. There was a cheap lunch for less than $2, served at a restaurant across the street. On Tuesday, he showed up early to lunch, about 12:30, and was the first one there. The waiter sat him down and turned on the TV, as he normally did for customers, but

Mark asked him to turn it off again, since he liked the tranquility. He regretted this as he sat alone in the restaurant, feeling bad every time he accidentally made eye contact with the waitress who hurried to check on the food.

He made sure his friends knew where his new apartment was and, that Thursday, had one of the biggest groups, eight Peruvians, come to the Bible study. They sat on Mark's two cheap couches as Mark started a series of lessons on the book of Proverbs. He told them about the fear of the Lord being the beginning of wisdom and the importance of obeying God. Mark felt that his move to his new apartment had been what he needed for his ministry to start flourishing. He went to Esperanza again that Sunday so the other missionaries wouldn't bother him, and on the next Thursday he was happy to have six come to his study.

That Friday, August first, was the one-year anniversary of Mark being a missionary—five months in Costa Rica and seven in Peru—so Wheaton paid off the first quarter of his student loans. He had made major steps forward in making a place for himself among the people he wanted to work with, and he hoped that, in years to come, he would learn to identify with them even more and raise up leaders from among them. He would someday fondly recall this time of difficulty and all the good his sacrifices had achieved.

During the prayer meeting that night, he thought about how far he had come, from appearing indistinguishable from those other missionaries who were seated around him to now identifying with the locals in a way none of them did. He was sure to overcome the current troubles with time, and the other missionaries would have to admit he had sacrificed what was needed to be the best missionary.

Mark left the prayer meeting shortly after it finished rather than spend time hanging out with the rest of the missionaries. Now that he went to Esperanza instead of Divino Redentor, the only time he saw the director was at the prayer meetings. They hadn't had one of their monthly planning and review meetings since the director made Mark leave Divino Redentor. Apparently, neither of them really wanted to make it happen.

The next day, he ate rotisserie chicken with his friends at a *pollería* restaurant he hadn't been to before. He had begun to make it a point to eat the salads with his meals, even though every other gringo had warned him not to. Mark knew people got food poisoning from salads on occasion, but he wanted to develop an immune system that could handle it. He wanted to enjoy all Peruvian food and made efforts to like everything. Once, while he had been eating cebiche, the raw fish soaked in lemons and onions, the waiter came over and commented on his eating different Peruvian foods, concluding, "You're more Peruvian than some Peruvians."

José, Luis, and Pedro came by Mark's apartment afterwards, but it wasn't long before he started to feel sick. José and Pedro admitted they felt a little bad, but Mark got the brunt of it and began to vomit. As he got worse, José offered to take him to his family's place so they could take care of him there. Though Mark felt terrible physically, it was the kind of offer he had long been waiting for, and he gladly accepted. He already had his keys, cell phone, and some change in his pocket, so he put some clothes along with his toothpaste and toothbrush in his backpack and carefully locked up his apartment.

At José's apartment, Mark lay down on the couch in the front room to rest. The others joked about putting him in the room of José's sister Milagros, but finally José offered him his own bed. They led him first past the curtain and into the dining room. There was a large table covered by a tablecloth with wooden chairs around it. This room was still relatively well kept, but wasn't as pristine or well decorated. They pointed out the location of the bathroom and then entered the boys' room, where José and his two nephews normally slept. There were three beds filling up the majority of the room, leaving little room to walk. On the wall were several posters, a small picture of *El Señor de los Milagros* painting, and an advertisement calendar of women in bikinis. There were a few spots on the wall where the paint was starting to peel. The floor was somewhat cluttered with school papers and clothes, and the room was lit by a bare light bulb that came out of the ceiling. It smelled like a room guys slept in. Mark lay down in the bed, and they covered him with an abundance of blankets. He slept fitfully that night, having to drag himself to the bathroom several times. He noticed that the nephews' beds remained empty; they must have been made to sleep elsewhere.

The next morning, Sunday, seeing that Mark was still sick, José's mom went out and brought back her aunt. The aunt, a short old woman whose face was creased with deep wrinkles, was a *curadora*, a traditional healer, and as soon as Mark heard this, he was afraid of what witchcraft she might use on him.

"What is she going to do?" asked Mark anxiously.

"I'm going to figure out what's wrong with you and fix it," the old woman replied simply.

She began poking and rubbing his stomach. Mark watched her intently, looking for any sign of an incantation. He felt vulnerable and weak.

The aunt pulled out an egg and started to wave it over Mark. He knew this was a traditional divination technique, to wave an egg over someone, break it open, and "read" what the problem was.

Mark groaned, "Stop! Please. I don't want your witchcraft!"

The aunt held back the egg, offended.

"My witchcraft?" she asked. "This is how we heal. These are the traditions from our ancestors from before the Spanish arrived."

"I don't want your traditions!" said Mark.

"Would you rather have one of your American doctors?" asked the aunt.

"I would rather have nothing," said Mark quietly. "I'll be okay by myself."

The aunt left the room, clearly offended, and Mark could hear them arguing in the family room. Eventually the aunt left and the family came back, but they didn't say anything about what had happened.

At about 11:00 AM, the missionary couple called Mark's cell phone. He explained that he hadn't come to church because he was sick. They said they would stop by his apartment, but Mark told them he was being taken care of at a friend's apartment, glad he wouldn't have to tell them about his move.

After an early dinner of chicken soup with rice, Mark was well enough to walk back to his own apartment to sleep. When he and José got there, he only had to turn the key one half turn, though he was sure he had bolted it with three turns. He opened up the door, and they saw papers, garbage, and couch cushions strewn around the apartment.

Whoever had done it had dug through everything, from the sofa and bed to the dresser, taking all they could. Anything of value was gone: Mark's CDs, CD player, laptop, wallet, debit card, camera, cell phone charger, most of his clothes, and even his English Bible. Mark grabbed one of the couch cushions from the floor and put it back on the couch so he could sit down. His first thought was about how to keep from losing all the money from his debit card, but he tried to ignore that for now. José was very angry and began talking about what he would do if he ever found out who did this, but Mark made him stop. He said that in a way it was good he'd been robbed, since it would help him to not be dependent on material things.

José helped Mark pick up the sheets off the floor and make the bed, though the comforter was gone. Mark no longer felt any shame in letting José see his room. He went to a phone booth to call his parents so they could tell the bank about the debit card being stolen. He told his parents he was feeling rather sick, but didn't let them know anything else had been stolen. After going out to buy a blanket, some crackers, and bottled water, Mark convinced José he would be okay for the rest of the day. José said he would be back the next morning.

Mark lay down in bed, but he kept thinking about the door, which wasn't bolted shut. He got up slowly and walked to the door to bolt it shut and returned to bed. The outside world felt like an enemy. He managed to sleep for five hours and, when he woke up again, everything was dark. He was feeling somewhat better, so he got up and flipped the light switch, but the light bulbs had been stolen as well.

The next morning Mark got up and looked through the socks and underwear scattered on the floor and found the old sock he had hidden $100 in when he had first come to Peru. It had survived his moves and was missed during the robbery. He drank water, ate some crackers, and lay back down on the bed. He wanted to put on his Keith Green CD, but both the CD and CD player had been stolen. José came by, and they went out together to change Mark's $100 into Peruvian *soles*. That would pay for food for a few weeks, but he would need to get money out of his bank account to pay for rent. He and José bought fresh bread and jam and went back to the apartment to eat it.

He had to watch his money carefully that week. At an Internet café, he found out he only had a couple hundred dollars left in his account, and he still didn't have a way of retrieving it. On Wednesday Mark watched his cell phone slowly die. He didn't want to spend the money to buy a new charger. He didn't leave the apartment much, and only Carlos came to the Bible study on Thursday, but Carlos didn't provide much comfort. Mark longed to start over with a new set of friends, but he immediately felt guilty for letting that thought even enter his head.

He skipped the prayer meeting Friday since the taxi was too expensive, and then, on Sunday, skipped the Esperanza service as well. That evening Mark heard a knock at the door and, assuming it was one of his friends, answered it. To his surprise, it was the mission director, who came in without waiting for an invitation.

"I called many times, left many messages, and finally spent all day trying to find out where you disappeared to," said the director. Mark quickly glanced back to make sure his bedroom door was shut so the director wouldn't see that everything had been taken.

"Do you know how many people are worried about you and praying for you?" the director continued. "Well, I better call them and let them know you're alive."

The director pulled out his cell phone. He paced back and forth by the window as he talked.

"Hi, honey… Yes, I found Mark. He seems to be okay, but he's living in a different apartment building. Can you let everyone else know that he's okay? Thanks … No, I don't know what I'm going to do with him," said the director, glancing at Mark. "I'll let you know what happens. Love you. Bye."

The director closed his cell phone and sat down heavily on Mark's cheap, used couch. Mark remained standing and said nothing.

"Well, I'm here to tell you that this is your last chance. If you don't do exactly what I tell you from now on, your time in Peru is over."

"*Cómo?*" asked Mark, refusing to speak in English, "How can you make me leave?"

"First, we are paying you, or at least we were," said the director, continuing in English. "You will not receive any more money from us unless you show that you are ready to listen."

"I'll find another way to get money," replied Mark confidently, still in Spanish.

"Second, you got your visa through us. I will call the Peruvian government and tell them that we are no longer responsible for you and want your visa canceled."

"You can't do that!" shouted Mark.

"Why not?" asked the director.

"I'm called to be a lifelong missionary!"

"Are you sure?" asked the director.

"Yes! God has not called me to be a conformist American. He has called me to do His work in a foreign country."

"Well, unless God intervenes, I'm going to send you back to the States."

"What about Wheaton paying off my debts?" asked Mark.

"Apparently Wheaton won't be paying off all your debt," said the director. "You'll have to get a regular job in the States to pay it off. Maybe you will learn to serve God humbly in a normal job."

"I don't want to do an unimportant, normal job. I want to do special work for God!"

"A missionary is no more spiritual than someone who honestly serves Jesus in an average job in the States."

"I'm sure that's what they tell themselves," replied Mark bitterly.

The director paused before continuing. "You have been very difficult to work with. I sincerely hope you learn something through all of this."

"You certainly haven't been perfect," said Mark. "Look at the problems in your mission church. Look at how you've isolated yourself from authentic Peruvians. Look at all the expensive, *pitucas*, houses you missionaries live in."

"Not all of our missionaries live like that. The Tillmans live at the orphanage in El Centro, the Dawsons live in …"

"I don't care about them," interrupted Mark. "You have still failed to follow God when He asks us to give up our comforts!"

The director frowned and looked at the floor intensely. "I know I've done a lot of things wrong, and I ask for forgiveness." He slowly looked up and gave a half smile. "Thank God that Jesus forgives, right?"

"That's no excuse for failure," replied Mark.

The director's smile vanished, and he looked straight at Mark and said, "I am buying you a plane ticket for Tuesday night. I'll settle any bills that remain with what's left of your mission account. All that you are required to do is be packed and ready to leave Tuesday after lunch. Is there anything you need to hold you over until then?"

Mark didn't respond.

"Then I'll see you Tuesday afternoon," said the director.

As Mark watched the director get up and walk out the door, a sense of panic rose up within him. With the loud bang of the door, he felt like he had just fallen into some hunter's trap. Mark stood up and began pacing. What could he do? He didn't have much money after getting robbed. He would have to get new supporters on his own, or maybe a job. Worse was the visa. He could only get a tourist visa by leaving the country, which was expensive to do, and then it would only last three months. Also, would Wheaton continue to pay off his debt if he wasn't with an official mission? It was as if the Universe itself was conspiring against him, hemming him in, behind and before.

Mark began thinking through who could help him out. The Peruvians he knew didn't have the resources to help him, and the other missionaries wouldn't help. He thought maybe Nathan could tell him what to do. Mark realized he didn't have Nathan's number; it had been on his laptop. He went to an Internet café, found the number in an e-mail, and wrote it on the back of a receipt. He went into the phone booth and dialed. It went to voice mail. He could feel despair closing in on him, but he decided to try again after five minutes. Mark counted the time on his watch and dialed again, and this time Nathan answered.

Nathan sounded surprised to hear Mark and said he was in a meeting.

"I really need to talk to someone," said Mark, his desperation coming through in his voice.

"Well, I guess I can miss a few minutes of the meeting," said Nathan. "What's going on?"

Mark told about what had happened with the director, the apartment and the robbery, and how he was now being forced to leave. As he spoke, he was surprised to find his voice flying up in pitch, out of control, and breaking into short sobs. He felt strangely disconnected from the emotion coming out in his voice, and he kept apologizing and having to pause before continuing.

"Man, that's rough," said Nathan after Mark had finished telling his story.

"What should I do?" asked Mark, wiping his nose with his hand.

"It doesn't sound like you're left with much choice, does it?" asked Nathan.

"But I can't leave!" said Mark. "I'm called to be a missionary."

"Well," said Nathan. "I can't tell you what's going to happen, but you can count on Jesus. He will work everything out for good in the end, no matter how bad it gets in the meantime."

"But how do I get out of this mess?"

"I don't know the answer to that one," said Nathan. "Only Jesus knows; ask Him. But listen, man, I've got to get back to this meeting. Can you call me back a little later?"

"I guess," said Mark. "When should I call?"

"Try in a couple hours or later tonight, which I guess would be your morning."

"I'll try to call then," said Mark.

"Sounds good," said Nathan. "I'll be praying for you, and I'll talk to you again soon."

"Okay," said Mark.

He listened as Nathan hung up on him. He had been hoping to get some practical course of action from Nathan. Mark returned home and went to bed, too tired to try again that night. He felt like he was in a nightmare where some inexorable force was chasing him and nothing he did could stop it.

Mark tried to call Nathan once Monday morning, but got a busy signal. He told himself that he would try again later or on another day.

José and Carlos came that afternoon, and Mark had to tell them the director was trying to make him leave. They both offered to call the director and yell at him, but he told them not to and told them about the director getting his visa canceled. They offered to help buy bus tickets for him go to Chile every three months to maintain a tourist visa, but Mark would've felt bad taking their money.

That evening, seeing nowhere else to turn, Mark went to the Internet café and called his parents. His mom answered the phone and sounded relieved when she found out it was him. When his father got on another phone, Mark's mom asked if he was okay.

"No, not really," said Mark.

Mark's mom took a breath and began, "We've been trying to call you. Mr. Bridges called us last night, and ..."

"The mission director?" asked Mark, flinching at the name.

"Yes," she said. "Mr. Bridges told us that he is kicking you out of the mission." Her voice broke, and she couldn't continue.

Mark's dad picked it up. "Did you really move into a dangerous neighborhood without telling anyone?"

Mark felt cornered. "Well, my Peruvian friends knew, but the director ..."

"Why did you do that?" he asked.

"The director doesn't understand," said Mark, exasperated. "I need to live with the people I am working with."

"Not if it's dangerous you don't," said his dad.

"I'm not afraid of danger," said Mark.

"That's 'cause you've been lucky. So far the worst that's happened is a lost credit card," said his dad.

"That's not true," said Mark quietly. "I lost my credit card when my apartment was broken into."

"What?" asked his mom. "Are you all right?"

"Yes. I'm fine. I just had most of my stuff stolen," said Mark. "That's actually what I called about. If I find a way to get money, I can still make this work and stay here."

"Stay there?" asked his dad.

"Yes," said Mark, fighting back tears. "I'm called to be a lifelong missionary here."

"Well, we're not going to help you stay," said Mark's dad.

"Please come home, Mark," said his mom, still crying.

"Well, can you at least help me pay for the plane ticket?" asked Mark. "It will cost about $600."

"Oh, you don't have to worry about that," said Mark's mom. "Mr. Bridges said that he already bought you a plane ticket to come home tomorrow night."

Mark suddenly felt ashamed. He had tried to trick his parents into giving him money. They weren't aware that Mark already knew he wouldn't have to pay for a plane ticket. For a second Mark loathed what he had just done.

"Please come home, Mark," pleaded his mom.

"Okay," he said softly.

"We'll be ready to pick you up at the airport on Wednesday morning," said his dad.

"Okay," said Mark.

"Be careful," said his mom. "I love you."

"Thanks," said Mark.

Mark hung up the phone. He returned home, lay down on the couch, and closed his eyes. That conversation had not gone as planned. He knew that, barring a miracle, he was returning to the United States of America on the following night. He opened his eyes to look around and think about what he should pack, but he remembered that all he had were some clothes and a few small things that hadn't been stolen. Mark closed his eyes again and covered his head with a pillow, feeling that he was slowly being forced to submit to some horrible new reality.

José came by the next morning, and Mark told him he was really leaving the country. José tried to argue, but Mark wouldn't let him.

"When will you come back?" asked José.

"I hope soon," said Mark.

José asked for Mark's U.S. address.

"We will write each other a lot, no?" asked José.

"Claro," lied Mark sadly.

José stayed with him the whole day and even took him to his home for breakfast. Mark knew José was just trying to keep him company, but he was depressed and wanted to be left alone. He put what little he still owned in a big plastic trash bag and tied it shut.

Around two o'clock the director showed up at his apartment. Mark was ashamed to have to explain why he had only one bag of possessions. When the director found out he didn't have a passport anymore, he said, "You're kidding, right? Any other important details you've neglected to tell me about?"

"No," said Mark quietly. "I think that's all of them."

"Okay. We have to move fast to get you a new passport in time."

Mark said good-bye to José, then the director sped them off across town to the heavily guarded U.S. embassy. He felt like he was already separated from Lima as he watched the city go by through the SUV's windows. The director had to lend Mark money to pay the extra fee for the embassy to rush a new passport. They went back to the rental offices of the two apartments where Mark had lived in El Centro and the director paid everything that was still owed. They went back to the embassy, picked up the new passport, and the director then took Mark to his house to have dinner with him and his wife.

They didn't say much during dinner. The director's wife politely asked Mark a few questions, but he barely answered and mostly just stared at his plate, occasionally taking a bite of the casserole.

After dinner, they went to the airport, and as they waited in the long line to check in, Mark couldn't believe any of it was happening. He couldn't believe he was never going to walk the streets of Peru again, or see his friends again. He felt like he would wake up the next morning in his cheap apartment for another day in El Centro. He felt foolish checking in his single garbage bag of possessions, leaving him with no carry-on.

After checking in, they went up the escalator and past the food court. Passing between a McDonald's on the right and a small McDonald's desserts store on the left, Mark saw the restaurants as sentries welcoming him into the land of commercialism. He paid the airport tax, went through security, and boarded the plane.

He was shocked by the loud, brash Americans who were taking their seats near him. They laughed about their jobs and possessions, and he couldn't help feeling that they were talking louder to hide how shallow their lives were.

A middle-aged woman sat next to Mark and tried to engage him in conversation.

"Hi! My name is Mary. What's your name?"

"Mark," he mumbled.

"Where are you headed?"

"My parents'."

"Oh. I'm headed back to Austin, Texas. What have you been doing in Peru?"

"Being a missionary," he said, hardly loud enough to be heard.

"Well good for you, doing the Lord's work," said the woman cheerfully. "I've been here on vacation with my husband, who got seated a few rows back there, and we went to Machu Picchu. It was the most incredible thing I've ever seen. Did you get to see it?"

"No."

Mark turned away, and by the time the plane took off the woman eventually gave up on talking to him. He sat quietly with his thoughts for the remainder of that flight and managed to avoid any conversation whatsoever on the second flight from Mexico City to Minneapolis-Saint Paul.

As the plane began to descend into the Twin Cities, the reality of what was happening hit him. He had failed. His dream, his calling as a lifelong missionary, was sputtering out like a fire built on nothing. Out of the window, he saw the gray parking lot of America approach. He would be forced to find a way of life alien to him, which he had long refused to see—a life lost in a crowd, a life as just another piece of gravel. He was returning prematurely to a land he thought he had left forever. Worse, he returned with fifty-six thousand dollars of debt. *Jesus,* thought Mark in horror, *what am I going to do now?*

For complementary study guides and discussion
questions, go to www.matthewdohyer.com, click on
Study Materials, and use the following log-in:

username: printedition
password: elcentro

Made in the USA
Lexington, KY
29 July 2017